Pokémon

Let It Snow!

**Adapted by
Tracey West**

OFFICIAL
Pokémon
MASTER'S
CLUB

SCHOLASTIC INC.
New York Toronto London Auckland Sydney
Mexico City New Delhi Hong Kong Buenos Aires

Published by Scholastic Inc.
90 Old Sherman Turnpike, Danbury, CT 06816.

SCHOLASTIC and associated logos are trademarks and/or registered trademarks of
Scholastic Inc.

ISBN 0-439-72193-8

First Scholastic Printing, June 2005

Togepi and Pikachu were on
a new adventure.

Their friend Todd was looking
for a very rare Pokémon—Articuno.

Ash, Misty, and Brock wanted
to help their friend.

Brock called
on his Golbat.

Golbat used Supersonic to look
for Articuno.

Golbat found something. But
it was not Articuno.
"It is Jigglypuff!" Misty cried.
"But Jigglypuff is
frozen."
Ash called on
Cyndaquil to melt
the ice.

"Jigglypuff, do you know where Articuno is?" Misty asked.

Jigglypuff pointed to the top of Snow Top Peak. "We can climb to the top," Ash said.

Team Rocket was climbing
Snow Top Peak, too.

But Team Rocket was in trouble.
They were stuck on a ledge in a
snowstorm.

"We are going to freeze!"
cried Jessie.

Just then a Pokémon flew down
from the sky. Snow fell all around it.
"What is that?" cried Meowth.

The Flying Pokémon took Team
Rocket to a safe place.

Ash and his friends climbed up Snow Top Peak. They did not know that Team Rocket was nearby.

Soon Ash and his friends came to a Pokémon Center. Officer Jenny was there, too.

Todd could not wait to find
Articuno.

"I want to take a picture of it,"
Todd told Officer Jenny.

"Articuno is a rare Pokémon,"
said Jenny. "Not many people have
seen one."

Nurse Joy
overheard them
talking.

"You have come
to the right place,"
she said. "Articuno
lives on Snow Top
Peak. It helps
people who
are in trouble."

Nurse Joy and Officer Jenny led them all outside.

There, they saw a statue of Articuno. "That is cool!" said Ash.

Suddenly the wind began to blow. Snow began to fall.

Then the wind and snow stopped.
Jessie, James, and Meowth had
fallen to the ground with the snow.
"It is Team Rocket!" Ash cried.

Team Rocket told their story
of being rescued.

"Articuno must have helped them,"
Todd guessed. "Just like
Nurse Joy told us."
Todd wanted to
go find Articuno right
away. So he left.

Ash and his friends ran after
Todd. They all climbed up the peak.
Jigglypuff followed them.

"Oh no!" Misty cried. "It is
snowing again!"

The snow fell harder and harder. The friends could not see anything but white snow.
"*Pika! Pika!*" said Pikachu.

"What is it, Pikachu?" Ash asked.
All of a sudden a Pokémon flew right in front of them.

"Articuno!" someone cried.

The friends stopped. It was Todd—
and Articuno!

Ash took a step closer. Articuno cried out.

Then Ash looked down. They were about to walk off a cliff! They could not see their way because of the snow.

Articuno had saved them!
Todd tried to take a picture of
Articuno. But something attacked
the Pokémon!

It was Team Rocket!

"Why are you doing this?" Ash asked them. "Articuno helped you."

"Now Articuno can help us again," said James. "It can let us bring it back to the Boss!"

Team Rocket called on Arbok and Weezing to battle Articuno.

Arbok attacked Articuno with Poison Sting.

The Poison Sting did not hurt Articuno. The rare Pokémon fought back with Ice Beam.

Jessie called on Wobbuffet.
It used a move called Mirror Coat.
It sent the Ice Beam right back
at Articuno.

Articuno moved just in time.
The reflected Ice Beam hit the snowy
peak of the mountain. Big chunks of
ice broke off.

The ice landed on the cliff that
Ash and Todd were standing on! The
cliff broke! Ash and Todd
went tumbling down.

"Pika!" cried Pikachu. It jumped
off the cliff to help Ash. Jigglypuff
jumped off, too.

Suddenly Jigglypuff puffed up.
It floated to the ground with Pikachu
on its back. They found Ash and Todd.

"Hey, we are not hurt," Ash said.

Then they realized
what happened.

"Articuno must
have saved us from
falling!" Todd said.

Then Team Rocket came crashing down. They did not want to give up.

Arbok attacked Articuno with Poison Sting.

Weezing attacked Articuno with Sludge.

Articuno used Blizzard.
Cold snow fell from the sky.
A strong wind hit Team Rocket.
    "We are blasting off again!" they
yelled. The wind took Team Rocket
far, far away.

The sun came out. Articuno
twinkled in the icy light.

Todd snapped a picture. "That is just the picture I wanted," he said with a smile.

Brock and Misty rode up on a snowmobile.

"Are you all right?" Misty asked.

"We sure are," Ash said. "Thanks to Articuno!"

"Pikachu!" agreed Pikachu.

Who's That
Ice
Pokémon?

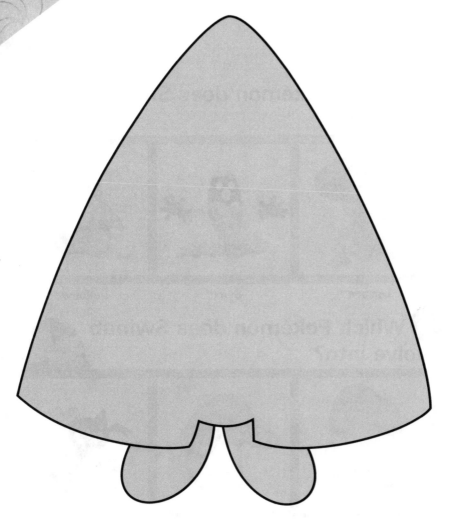

See page 45 or your
Ice & Fighting Pokédex
for the answer.

Icy Evolutions

Do you know which Ice Pokémon each of the following Pokémon evolve into?

1. Which Pokémon does Smoochum evolve into?

Lombre™   Jynx™   Delibird™

2. Which Pokémon does Swinub evolve into?

Piloswine™   Phanpy™   Sneasel™

3. Which Pokémon does Shellder evolve into?

Cloyster™

Regice™

Omanyte™

4. Which Pokémon does Seel evolve into?

Articuno™

Mudkip™

Dewgong™

5. Which Pokémon does Snorunt evolve into?

Shelgon™

Glalie™

Lapras™

39

Check page 45, your *Ice & Fighting Pokédex*, or your *Ultimate Sticker Book* for the answers.

Battle Time!

Now it is your turn to battle! Read about each battle below. Then pick the best Pokémon to use against your opponent. In each battle, all of the Pokémon are the same level.

1. Put on your parka! Your opponent is Regice, an Ice Pokémon. Which Pokémon can best stand up to its freezing attacks?

Donphan™
(Ground)

Quilava™
(Fire)

Meganium™
(Grass)

2. Your opponent throws out the Fighting Pokémon Machop. Which Pokémon will last the longest against it?

Sudowoodo™
(Rock)

Mightyena™
(Dark)

Koffing™
(Poison)

3. Your opponent is Pineco, a Bug Pokémon. Which of these Pokémon has the best chance of winning?

Ekans™
(Poison)

Seedot™
(Grass)

Kirlia™
(Psychic)

Check page 45 or your
Pokédex books for the answers.

Double Trouble

Some Fighting Pokémon have more than just Fighting moves. Which of these Pokémon are Dual Types?

1.

Breloom™   Makuhita™   Primeape™

2.

Mankey™   Tyrogue™   Poliwrath™

3. Hariyama™   Meditite™   Machop™

4. Hitmonlee™   Heracross™   Machamp™

5. Machoke™   Hitmontop™   Combusken™

Check page 45, your *Ice & Fighting Pokédex,* or your *Ultimate Sticker Book* for the answers.

Ice & Fighting Pokémon Jokes

What does Articuno eat for lunch?

Iceburgers!

Why did the Combusken cross the road?

To prove it wasn't chicken!

What is Primeape's favorite food?

Chocolate chimp cookies!

Where does Regice keep its money?

In a snow bank!

What do you get when you cross a Glalie with a Raticate?

Frostbite!

What does Machop love to eat?

Kung food!

Answers

Page 37: Who's That Ice Pokémon?
Snorunt!

Pages 38–39: Icy Evolutions
1. Jynx
2. Piloswine
3. Cloyster
4. Dewgong
5. Glalie

Pages 40–41: Battle Time!
1. Quilava (Fire beats Ice)
2. Koffing (Poison beats Fighting)
3. Ekans (Poison beats Bug)

Pages 42–43: Double Trouble
1. Breloom (Grass/Fighting)
2. Poliwrath (Water/Fighting)
3. Meditite (Fighting/Psychic)
4. Heracross (Bug/Fighting)
5. Combusken (Fire/Fighting)